I'M GETTING A SHARK!

BY BRADY SMITH

 Nancy Paulsen Books

For
Harper,
Holt,
and every kid
who loves animals
and has a desire
to protect them

Nancy Paulsen Books
An imprint of
Penguin Random House LLC, New York

Visit us online at penguinrandomhouse.com

Library of Congress Cataloging-in-Publication Data
Names: Smith, Brady, 1971– author, illustrator. Title: I'm getting
a shark! / Brady Smith. Other titles: I am getting a shark! Description:
New York: Nancy Paulsen Books, [2021] | Summary: "A shark-obsessed
little girl is convinced she is getting a pet shark for her birthday"—
Provided by publisher. Identifiers: LCCN 2020019297 |
ISBN 9780593111123 (hardcover) | ISBN 9780593111147 (ebook)
| ISBN 9780593111130 (ebook) | Subjects: CYAC: Sharks—
Fiction. | Pets—Fiction. | Birthdays—Fiction. | Classification:
LCC PZ7.1.S596 Im 2021 | DDC [E]—dc23 LC record
available at https://lccn.loc.gov/2020019297

Manufactured in China by RR Donnelley Asia
Printing Solutions Ltd.

ISBN 9780593111123
1 3 5 7 9 10 8 6 4 2

Design by Marikka Tamura
Text set in New Century Schoolbook LT Std.
The illustrations were done with a No. 2 pencil, an eraser, a
Faber-Castell artist pen, watercolors, and some digital tweaks in Procreate.

I'm so excited, Ralphie!
I heard Mom tell Dad
I'm getting a shark
for my birthday!

Yikes!

Are you sure?

Ralphie

Yes! And there are so many different types. I wonder what kind I'm going to get!

BIG ONES

LITTLE ONES

ROUND ONES

ZIGZAGGY

STRIPED

LONG ONES

CHECKERED

Whoa, kiddo,
slow down!
Let's try and think
this through.

SPOTTED

Some even
glow in
the dark!

Okay. I'm thinking it's a whale shark. They are really cool!
I would invite all my friends over for a pool party!

Wait a minute. We'd
need a bigger pool.
Whale sharks are
the biggest fish in
the ocean—excluding
whales, of course, which
are really mammals.

Or maybe I'm getting a cute little dogfish shark! We could even open up a dogfish grooming salon!

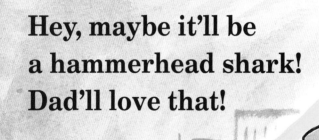

Hey, maybe it'll be a hammerhead shark! Dad'll love that!

Or a megamouth shark. Ha-ha, isn't that a funny name?

$1 to look inside!

Or a cute little spotted cat shark!

I think you're missing my point here. Sharks are NOT meant to be pets . . .

SHARP
TEETH!
DO NOT
TOUCH!
(SERIOUSLY)

And I think you're forgetting the whole teeth thing. Some sharks have over three hundred teeth that are incredibly sharp—perfect for biting food and defending themselves. Which is another reason why a shark would NOT make a good pet!

Well, you have sharp teeth and you're a good pet.

Well, you've got a point there.

Hey, Ralphie, maybe I'm getting a bull shark!

A bull shark! Those are ferocious! Why in the world would you want a bull shark?!

Speaking of being nice, maybe you could help the sharks. Did you know they've been around for millions of years, since dinosaur times? But they could become extinct too.

I like sharks!
I like them!
I like the lemon shark!
The zebra shark!
The goblin shark!
The wobbegong shark!

OH, AND I LOVE

THE GREAT WHITE!

Wow. That's an awfully small box.

Wait! WHAT IS THIS?
It's a *picture* of
a shark! I wanted a
REAL SHARK!!!

Adoption CERTIFICATE

Honey, it *is* a real shark.
It's an adoption certificate for a shark that is swimming in the ocean right now, happy and healthy. And you're helping it stay that way.

Thank you.

EXACTLY BEEN TRYING THIS WHOLE

Oh, sorry. I hear you now.
And I'm ready to help!

Did you know there are special organizations that let you help animals in need? You can support all kinds of cool animals! Lions, zebras, elephants, seals, turtles! Any animal you want to help, you can! Ask an adult to get you started and help an animal today!

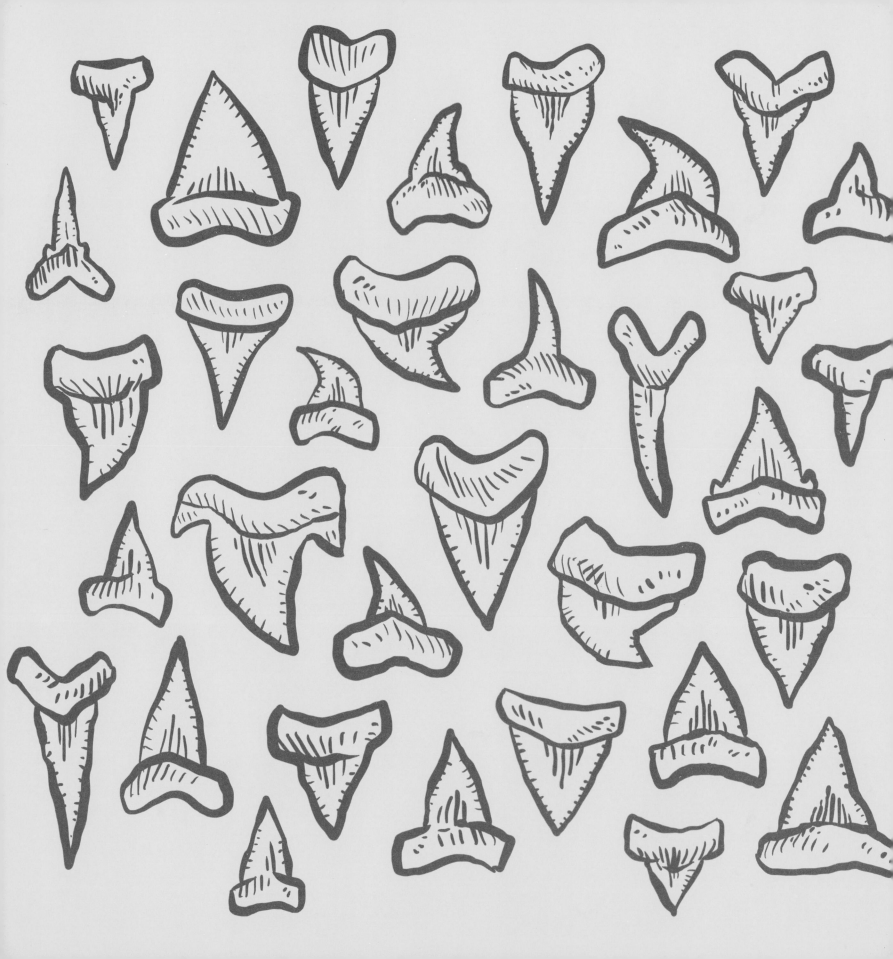